Stories of Strangers

Also by Simon Stuart and published by Ginninderra Press
Beauty in the Ruins

Simon Stuart

Stories of Strangers

Acknowledgements

'True north' was published in *Forty South Short Story Anthology 2015: The 10 Best Stories from the Tasmanian Writers' Prize 2015*

'A cute distraction' was published in *1,000 Words or Less – Flash Fiction Collection 2* in 2016

Thanks to Jane-Marie Stuart, Michael de Valle, John Irving, Stephen Matthews and to the good people who supported *Beauty in the Ruins*

Stories of Strangers
ISBN 978 1 76109 335 7
Copyright © text Simon Stuart 2022
Cover image: Jane-Marie Stuart

First published 2022 by
GINNINDERRA PRESS
PO Box 3461 Port Adelaide 5015
www.ginninderrapress.com.au

Contents

True north

White noise hits fever pitch, the earth burns, you dive into the whirlpool, altitude fails, reason dissolves, it has a holocaustic effect on your compass. True north is lost.

*

'Where are we going?' you ask.

'You know,' Sam says and looks away.

You are sitting in a carriage on a train as it rattles over a bridge. You look out the window. The brick pylons that support the tracks stretch downwards, seemingly forever, into a gorge filled with water that encircles the vertical cliff face on the far side.

'Man equals decay,' booms a red-bearded man dressed in robes. He is standing at the front of the carriage facing and preaching at you all. 'The tracks that this train rides upon are rusting and the railway sleepers are brittle. You are a rotting sleeper, tethered to a rusting rail that was laid long before you came to be and that will exist long after you have returned to dust. The world owes you nothing.'

'Ignore him,' says Sam, taking your hand and giving it a gentle squeeze.

The train travels on through a grey, flat, barren landscape of dry long grass broken only by the occasional skeletal tree.

In time, a line of buildings can be seen on the horizon. The view out the window turns to broken concrete, rusting cables, steel, machinery, two-foot-high weeds and long-abandoned construction sites. The line of buildings are derelict, graffiti-scarred shops and factories.

At the station, you are all herded off the train by men in blue jumpsuits. A sea of sunken cheeks, bald skulls with tufts of grey hair, crooked anorexic bodies shuffle past you with downcast eyes. The men in blue jumpsuits direct you all to a waiting room that is already crowded with people.

You take a seat and turn to Sam and ask, 'What do we do now?'

'We wait,' Sam answers.

'What is this place?'

Sam looks at you with concern. 'You really don't remember, do you? Think of it as an island, cut off from the civilised, the mainland, reality. It backs onto the sea, surrounded by a moat. It is a necessary place. That railway bridge we crossed is the only way in or out.'

'Do we have to stay for long?'

'I hope not,' Sam says. 'Try and think about something else.'

But you can't, this place is all too familiar. There is a compound within you, a fortress where your strength is stored. Within it, there is a knowing that you have prevailed here before. But now, you are in danger again – you all are. A memory stirs. The people here are kind, but they hurt you.

'We have to get out of here,' you say.

'We can't, we have to wait,' replies Sam.

'I can't do this any more,' you say and hate yourself for it. 'There must be another way.'

Sam hesitates. It is the first crack in the facade, almost undetectable, but it's there and you can work away at it.

'I don't belong here. You have to help me.'

Sam slowly rises. 'There is another way. Follow me.'

Overgrown bushes and weeds run along the side of one of the old derelict factories. Sam stops walking and starts rummaging through them. You watch.

In time, from over Sam's shoulder, you see a hole at the base of the wall. Sam further parts the foliage, drops to all fours, then crawls through the opening. You follow. You are upright again in a vast cavernous deserted space of a onetime place of industry. Sam leads at a brisk pace to a door on the far wall and opens it. It reveals a staircase that only ascends. You step within the stairwell and Sam closes the door behind you. The open door had hidden another crude opening where the wall meets the floor.

Sam is down again, sitting now with legs thrust into the hole. 'Follow me and be careful.'

You hear Sam land. You drop to your backside and put your legs through into the abyss. You begin to lower yourself while still holding onto the opening, your feet dangle in the open space.

'Trust me,' says Sam, 'drop.'

Your feet, knees and spine jar as you land. You straighten up in a dark space, only lit by the natural light from the hole through which you dropped. Sam removes a thin torch from a pocket but doesn't turn it on. You set off together down a passageway that you eventually decide is descending. It grows darker and darker. Sam flicks the torch on; it throws more light than you expected. You pass by doors, the passage zigzags, the stench is putrid.

In time, the passage opens into a room where the only features of note are two five-foot circular openings. Sam stoops and steps through the closer of the two. You follow. The gradient is far steeper than before. Sam turns off the torch, you keep marching in single file. It is pitch-black.

Finally, there is a light in the distance.

Sam stops and says, 'Keep going towards the light,'

'Wait, you're not coming?' you say.

'You know I can't leave.'

'Please come with me.'

'And then what?'

'We can run from all of this. It can be like before.'

'I can't do that.'

'You can!'

'I don't get that option.'

'You always have a choice.'

'No, not always. I have to get back. They will be coming.'

'But we can still do all the things we always dreamt of. We don't have to keep living like this.'

'I do. I'll see you soon, I promise.'

'So you've decided. This is how it is.'

'It won't be forever. Nothing's forever,' Sam says, then turns and starts back up the pipe.

You stand alone in the dark. Long moments pass.

'Wait,' you call and start running after.

You arrive back in the room. All you can hear is your laboured breath. Your heart pounds at your ribs. In the blackness, you start back up the zigzagging hall.

You are back on the train platform. The old, broken, crooked people are still moving. Sam is nowhere to be seen. A man in a white coat is walking towards you.

You start backing away from him. 'Not again,' you say, 'not now, it's too soon.'

You turn and take off running. Leaping from the platform, you find yourself in a paddock with long grass, rocks, shrubbery, bespeckled with trees. You make it to the first shrub and dive behind it. You keep down, lying on your side, scrunched in a ball, trying to catch your breath. You hear shouting and people running.

A siren howls from the station platform, white pillars of light scan the night sky. Within the blackness behind one of the derelict buildings, you stand with your back pressed hard against the wall. You know you can't be seen. You are going to try and make your way back to the bridge. You concede it is not a great plan, but you can't hide out any longer. You are hoping Sam will be waiting for you there and you can both sneak back over it together.

A boot grinds the gravel and a thin light bursts into the blackness from between two of the buildings ahead. A figure appears and their torch starts darting and roaming through the darkness. Your position is no longer safe; you stiffen but know it's futile. The torch shoots past you and scans the wall further down. You move out and shrink down behind a line of long-forgotten crates and boxes. You brace yourself. The torch beam darts back and hits the wall where you've just been.

You are running as fast as you can. You can hear shouting; there is the pounding of boots behind you. The wind and cold make your vision blur, tears strike your ears. Where's Sam? I can't lose Sam, your mind screams. You can hear your pursuer getting closer. Something starts scratching at your back, you stumble, you thrust out your arms in an attempt to regather your balance. The pursuer is all but upon you, a force hits your back, you're losing your footing, you twist and hold onto the pursuer in an attempt to break your fall, their momentum takes you both to the ground and you crash to a stop.

The tackler is a dead weight above you, you are pinned beneath them. It was like this once before. You understand, you are trapped and you are powerless to stop it. There is beauty in knowing how it ends. You are ready, for you have prepared.

*

You're out, moving, looking straight ahead. Sam takes your hand; you could almost skip like a child as the endorphins of relief explode through your body. You are tempted to run, sprint as fast as you can, put the greatest distance between you both and that place. You can't and won't of course. This is the real world after all, reality. With every step, the fear and the tight chest recede. You arrive at the station, buy tickets and board the train.

'Are you doing OK?' Sam asks as you take a seat.

'I just feel so hopeless. Life stands still here. It goes on for the rest and stops for us.'

'Not this time,' Sam says and smiles.

The train slowly pulls away and you know you should be grateful. Many never get to leave this place. And you are grateful, and relieved, and happy. You look at Sam. Colour has returned to the face and you know that under the bandana, the hair is growing back, not as thick as it was. Every visit, Sam says you don't have to come. But you always do and always will.

'When do they want to see you again?' you ask.

'Three months,' says Sam as the train rattles over the bridge that separates that place from the mainland.

Belonging

She splashes water from the tap in the bathroom onto her face. Staring at her reflection in the mirror, she feels fresh, like it's a new world order. I've returned from a long quest. I was weary, I have rested and now somehow, I'm content, not unhappy. My story is told. Is my war really over? I'm not focused on the future. I'm not trying to build anything. I'm happy right now, just surviving. Have I evolved? It certainly feels different – I repeat, not unpleasant.

She returns to the living room and pours another drink. Life is sensory, just do everything you love every day. She takes a sip; the liquor burns the back of her throat. Perhaps I've misplayed some things in this life, but I'm free now and I'm creating space for new things to come in. I want a simpler, less anxious existence.

She turns the TV on and lies back on the couch. She pours another drink, her third. She scratches at an itch in her forearm. I should eat something. She stands and walks into the kitchen; her handbag is on one of the kitchen chairs. She takes out her phone. She takes a breath; I don't have to do this, she tells herself. She makes a call.

'Hi, Mum, it's me,' she says.

'Sally! Oh my God! Sally, how are you?' Her mother sounds older to her ear, almost a stranger, 'where are you?'

'Don't start. I just called to let you know I'm OK.'

'OK, I won't say anything. It's just so good to hear your voice. We've been so worried.'

'Don't start, Mum,' she says and feels all the old battles start to close in on her again. She feels as if she has lived a thousand years and yet still, just below the surface lurks the same old glowing ball, made up of all the old hurt and anger and bitterness and fear and regret.

Don't cry, she tells herself and don't get angry. 'I met a man, Mum.'

'That's wonderful!'

'He told me about how hard it can be for some of us to belong.'

'Oh, Sally,' her mother says and the tone in her voice has changed. It is the voice of her mother from long ago, warm, knowing. It transports her. In this moment, she is a little girl who has fallen and is hurt, and she is waiting for her mother to say something that just might make it all all right.

'Does anyone really ever find it easy?' her mother says.

With that, the glowing ball within her flares red, the water stirs, begins to percolate, boils, froths over, the tears and the howl of the beast explodes from within her, and she begins to sob down the line.

'My beautiful daughter,' she hears her mother say, 'the secret is, never stop trying.'

Never going to change

'They have opened the border,' says the younger soldier having just arrived at an isolated section of the wall. 'There are reports of people streaming through the checkpoints, climbing the fences, standing on the wall and smashing at it with sledge hammers.'

'What are our orders?' asks the old soldier on duty with him.

'No new orders.'

'Then nothing has changed.'

The younger soldier shakes his head. 'Do you want to know what the problem with your generation is?'

'Not from you.'

'You no longer recognise the truth, even when it is right before you.'

The old soldier grunts and lights another cigarette. He knows himself not to be a stupid man; when life brings you to a crossroads, pick a path, commit and be proud of your choice. Debates put forward by the young and the undecided are irrelevant and have long bored him. He understands that there is nuance in life, but ultimately, above all things, he values moral clarity. The indecisive are weak. Those who don't share his values are wrong. He sighs and says, 'Trust reason and believe that disrespect should be met with equal or greater force. That is truth enough for me.'

'That is not your truth.'

'It is the truth that I believe.'

'Then all you believe is propaganda. Written long ago by men who wanted us to think what they told us.'

'What you say changes nothing. We have our orders.'

'Orders… Spare me.'

'Careful, this is beginning to sound a lot like treason to me.'

'They programmed you well. Do you ever stop to think for yourself? Have you ever dared ask yourself the question, is our enemy really that bad?'

'I have no desire to debate ideas and ideologies with you.'

'Why not?'

'You are young. You know nothing of how the world really is.'

'And the world that you know will soon be gone. Your world and your values are collapsing and I feel for you, I do, because you have missed the point of life.'

'And you know the point, I take it?'

'I understand that the world is constantly changing, moving, evolving. I know that I may have to shed skins all the way along. At the very least, know when something that was successful has run its course. Yet you remain rigid in belief and therefore a sitting duck. You long ago chained yourself to an ideal and now you are rusted on. You are old and only getting slower and you are anchored to a lie. I ask a simple question – is our enemy really that bad? And you can't even consider the possibility.'

'Who do you think they are?' The old soldier explodes. 'Who do you think you are? They are our enemy and they hate us. Our fathers drew a line and we honour them by defending it. I am a soldier. Only the weak turn the other cheek, and if I turn the other cheek, our enemy prevails. In such a society, rapists, paedophiles and murderers would think it is Christmas. Is that the world you want?'

'Do you truly believe that?'

'I do not want to think about them. You are either with us or against us. I have my orders.'

'You are brainwashed and scared.'

'Brainwashed and scared am I? What kind of man are you? Our cause is worth bleeding for, our cause is worth dying for and, in what may be our darkest hour, you speak words of treason. You are gutless.'

'Your cause is dying. If you stand and fight with it, you may well get your wish. Our lives have been in a state of stalemate. It has to change, it has to end. Why can't you see that?'

'Ever heard of loyalty and conviction? Is there room for such qualities in your brave new world? Be careful, my young friend, that in your search for "liberty" you do not surrender belief and belonging. For you may end up with nothing.'

'If you stand with a system and the system is wrong, what good is your conviction and loyalty?'

'You are a traitor. Shut up, you get no more say.'

'You cannot tell me what to do. You are beaten. And you were beaten by an element that you were incapable of ever attaining. You have never been your own measure. You have never been your own man. At best, you tacitly joined the freeway of our father's ideals and philosophies which long ago ended in a cul-de-sac. You have spent your life guarding a dead end. The war is over. Are you going to spend the rest of your days mourning a lost cause?'

'Shut up.'

'You are holding on. Can't you feel the change? The world is moving forward with or without you. Do you truly still believe that things are never going to change?'

The old soldier has never forgotten what it was like being young, fragile and defenceless. His life then had constantly bombarded him with new material and choices. For the most part, he had been curious and brave. He had projected ambition onto an unwritten future. But he had also been afraid. So he built mental walls, fortifications, lines of demarcation, to hide behind and protect himself. But he hadn't been fully formed then, he had been in transition, a state of flux, and he had been in a hurry and he only got busier and more distracted, and time passed, and things changed, and he kept adapting. All the while 'projecting' new plans and therefore building 'new defences' on top of the previous ones. And everyone he had ever met was the same. He had forged relationships and, in doing so, became complicit in the plotting and building of their plans and their defences – their illusions…as they were in his… And they had parents and teachers who had been forged this same way…and he had parents and teachers…

Then he found a cause, and he believed, and he became a soldier. With that came duty and, with duty, a sense of peace. He stopped questioning. But not completely. In his darker moments, he secretly dreads that perhaps he's just been keeping himself a fingerprint in front all these years. And perhaps the day is coming when he will finally get run down… I can survive in a world of order, he would tell himself. Where there is duty and routine. Where there is a line to be held. Where clarity and decency prevail. But what if the people revolt and my house of cards gets caught in the crossfire? What if my whole life has been built on 'bad intel', or worse?

'Do you hear that?' asks the young soldier.

'What?'

'Singing?'

'No.'

The young soldier shakes his head and smiles, 'I am going to join them. Are you in or are you out? It is time to choose. Life is happening, right now.'

The old soldier lowers his eyes. 'There will be no retreat. I have my orders,' he says. He looks up and meets the young soldier's eyes again. 'But you can go.'

'Come with me.'

'I can't.'

'Why not?'

'I am too old to change.'

'You are never too old. You have got plenty of time.'

'Time is a funny thing. I have been me a lot longer than you have been you. Time changes who we are. You are smart, but you are young. You cannnot know yet what I know.'

'And what is that?'

'Time does not speed up, but that does not mean it is not running out.'

'So is this it for you, then? This is where you make your final stand, right here, right now, for this?'

'You have to believe in something.'

'A better tomorrow is all you have to believe in.'

'I know what I am. Security defines me,' the old soldier says. 'I said go. Leave.'

The young soldier shrugs, turns and walks off into night.

*

The old soldier is standing alone. He can hear the joyous, triumphant cheers and the singing in the distance now. 'Do you truly still believe that things are never going to change?' was the missing piece of the puzzle. 'I so want to, but I have to be so careful,' he tells himself. 'Soldiers seldom find peace in peace. Security has defined me, perhaps freedom can refine me?'

The pull is too strong… He is moving, placing one foot in front of the other. Where is my destination? he asks himself over and over. A better tomorrow is the answer, he thinks, as he arrives at a crowd of people marching together. They are smiling, singing, cheering, laughing. He enters that stream of people which in time joins the sea of humanity flowing, to and fro, east to west, north to south, back again and beyond.

The shipwreck

'My grandfather says I'm powerfully built,' was the last thing Anthony said before Ryan pushed him over.

'No, you're not,' Ryan said, towering over him. 'You're just a fat pig!'

I laughed, so did the rest of our gang. Then we all returned to chanting, 'Fat pig! Fat pig! Fat pig!' and Anthony began to cry.

Our teacher told us that in the coming weeks we would all have to give a short talk on 'a hobby'. When it came to Anthony's turn, he brought his viola into school. He told us that the viola was not a violin, that it was larger. He also showed us the bow and demonstrated how to apply the rosin to the horsehair. He told us that the rosin helps the horsehair grip the string. Ryan made a snoring sound. I tried hard not to laugh. Anthony said that he had been learning for almost two years and that his viola teacher likes him to practise every day for at least fifteen minutes.

'I have to wipe the excess rosin off the strings after every practice session with a rag and I hope to sit for my Grade 1 examination later this year. I will now play you a short piece,' Anthony announced and lifted his viola and wedged it between his shoulder and his chin.

He had hardly finished bowing the first note when Ryan started mooing like a cow. Everyone started to laugh. I even noticed the teacher smile. But I didn't laugh. I watched Anthony. I saw him close his eyes. He kept going. The laughter petered out and the piece came to an end. Silence. Before I realised what I was doing, I began to clap. On hearing the applause, Anthony stood tall then bowed deeply. The laughter exploded again. I kept clapping, I was the only one.

I received a tap on my shoulder. I turned round. It was Ryan. I stopped clapping.

He was smiling. 'Good one, Stevie,' he said.

The next morning, I arrived early at school and saw Anthony sitting by himself eating a sandwich and reading a book. There was no one around, so I went up to him and said, 'G'day, Anthony.'

He looked up a little startled, 'Oh, good morning, Stephen.'

'What are you reading?'

'A book about the history of sailing ships, it's very interesting.'

'Cool, sorry to disturb you.'

'No, that's perfectly fine.'

I was about to walk off, when I heard myself say, 'I enjoyed your performance yesterday.'

'That's very decent of you to say,' he paused and looked down. 'Stephen, I know it's terribly short notice, but you see, it's my birthday this weekend and Mother has been pestering me to invite a friend from school. Please feel free to say no, but I was just wondering if you might be available?'

'Ahhh.'

'Oh, I can see I've put you on the spot. I apologise.'

'No, don't be sorry. I'll have to check with my parents, but I'd love to come.'

'Oh, that is wonderful, thank you. My mother will be pleased.'

'I'll have to check,' I said, turned, and the very moment I started walking away, I began kicking myself. What have you done, you idiot? I can't get involved. I could and would get out of it of course, just tell him my parents said we already had plans. But I was angry because I had put myself into a bad situation. What if he wanted to hang out with me at recess and lunch now? The further I got away, the more it dawned on me that having to spend time with Anthony would be the least of my problems. How was Ryan going to react?

At recess, I didn't hang out with Ryan's gang. I didn't hang out with Anthony. I hid. When lunchtime came, I went out into the playground and had lunch with Ryan and the others. There was no sign of Anthony; no one mentioned him.

I couldn't get to sleep that night. I didn't know what to do. I was angry with Anthony for putting me in this position. I was terrified of what Ryan might do if he found out. Eventually, I started thinking about it all from Anthony's point of view.

I arrived at school early again the next morning, hoping to talk to Anthony before anyone saw me. Sure enough, he was sitting in the same place, but he wasn't reading. He saw me, waved, stood up and started waddling towards me. He really was chubby.

'Good morning, Stephen.'

'Good morning, Anthony.'

'By chance, did you get to speak to your parents about the weekend?'

'Yes, I did, Anthony. My mum and dad said we have no plans. So I'd be very happy to come to your birthday.'

'Oh, that is wonderful news. My mother has given me this note to give to your mother regarding the arrangements,' he said, removing a folded piece of paper from his trouser pocket.

I took it and stuffed it into my own pocket.

'It truly is splendid news that you can come. Thank you, Stephen.'

Dad drove me to Anthony's house, saying more than once that it was an expensive part of town.

'That's it, Dad,' I said, 'number 37.'

'Geez,' he said, pulling up to the curb, 'nice place. His old man must be worth a bob or two.'

'I think this is his grandparents' place,' I said. 'His mum and Anthony live here too.'

Dad lit a cigarette, 'I'll be back to get you at five thirty. Don't keep me waiting.'

'Sure, Dad,' I said and hopped out of his ute.

He drove off, tooting his horn once.

It looked more like a mansion than a house. There were garden beds filled with colourful plants and flowers. The lawn looked like it belonged at the bowling club. I walked up the path towards the front door. My mum had told me a long time ago and reminded me every time I went to a new place for the first time, to find something nice to say to the host about their home. It wasn't going to be difficult. I rang the doorbell and almost immediately, Anthony opened the front door. I'd only ever seen him in his school uniform. Today he was wearing a green cardigan over a blue skivvy tucked into brown-coloured corduroy pants.

'Welcome,' he said, smiling, 'we've been expecting you.'

'Thank you, Anthony,' I said.

A clock chimed from within the house.

'You're perfectly on time. Come in, come in.'

I followed him into the living room.

'This is my friend Stephen from school,' he announced to the room of five adults sitting around the coffee table.

A thin, pretty lady stood up straight away and walked towards me smiling and shook my hand. 'Hi, Stephen, I'm Mandy, Anthony's mum. I'm very pleased to meet you and we're all thrilled that you could make it.'

'I'm very pleased to meet you, Mrs Sherrill,' I said.

'Please, call me Mandy.'

'It's a lovely home you have here, Mandy,' I said.

'That's very polite of you to say. It's actually my parents' home. Stephen and I are staying here at the moment too.'

'Oh, sorry,' I said.

'Nothing to be sorry about. This is my mother and my father,' she said.

I looked for the two oldest people in the room. They nodded.

I smiled and said, 'It's a beautiful home you have here, Mr and Mrs Sherrill.'

'And finally,' Mandy said, 'this is my friend Luke.'

Luke had blond dirty-looking hair and was wearing a black leather jacket. He seemed a little out of place in this mansion with these people. 'How you are going, mate?' he said and stood, stepped towards me and shook my hand.

'Good, thanks. Pleased to meet you,' I said.

'Please take a seat,' Anthony said, gesturing to the brown leather couch with buttons punched into the cushions.

I said, 'This is for you,' and handed him the present I had for him and sat down.

Anthony sat down beside me and said, 'You shouldn't have,' and placed it beside him on the couch.

There were bowls of chips, nuts, cheese and biscuits on a plate laid out on the coffee table before us. A cork popped like a bullet, and Anthony and I were handed champagne glasses filled with champagne by Luke. Anthony assured me it was non-alcoholic. There was another pop and the adults' glasses were filled. We all stood again and toasted Anthony for his birthday.

'I can't believe my little boy is twelve,' Mandy said.

Then the six of us began chatting. I didn't say much. Anthony's grandfather asked me if I liked sport. I said yes, cricket and footy. He nodded; he seemed to approve. His grandmother asked if I played a musical instrument. I told her that we owned a piano, my mother used to play and that I liked to play on it a little. Mandy told Anthony to open my gift.

He read the card first, smiled and muttered, 'Most thoughtful.'

My mum had asked me what his interests were. I had told her that I had no idea, but then remembered that he played the viola. I had then had to explain to dad that the viola was actually bigger than a violin. I also told them that he was reading a book about sailing ships. So Dad had taken me to the local toy shop and we had bought him a medium-sized build-it-yourself model of a sailing ship.

'Oh, Grandad,' Anthony said once he had removed the paper. 'Look what Stephen got me.'

His grandfather smiled at me and said, 'What do you say, Anthony?'

'Thank you, Stephen, truly, a most thoughtful gift. My grandfather and I share a passion for all things nautical.'

'You're welcome,' I said.

Everybody made a fuss about the model ship. Then the plans for the afternoon were discussed. Anthony, Mandy, Luke and I were going to drive to have a picnic down by the bay. It was a sunny day, and everybody agreed it was the perfect day for it.

We waved goodbye to Anthony's grandparents and the four of us set off in Luke's old blue car. Anthony and I sat in the back seat. He whispered to me that the car was an Alfa Romeo, and that Luke was very fond of it. We took off and it sounded like a racing car revving high through the gears. We all chatted. I noticed Luke only ever called Mandy 'Beautiful.' He cracked jokes. I was starting to think that Luke was really cool.

We arrived at the picnic spot. There was a rusted brown shipwreck poking out of the water, not far out to sea. Anthony and Luke were fascinated by it. Luke used up a whole roll of film on his camera that afternoon. Every shot had Mandy in it, or Anthony and Mandy. He even took a couple of photos with Anthony, Mandy and me. Most of them had the rusty old shipwreck in the background.

'Tell me, Anthony,' I asked between bites of my sandwich, 'why are you so interested in this shipwreck?'

'That's a good question, Stephen,' he said and placed his plate down on the ground. 'My grandfather ignited my curiosity in all things nautical. He once said to me about shipwrecks, imagine you are the captain in the last desperate moments spent on board a ship that's about to sink. Knowing that you are the person responsible for the fate of everyone onboard and that it was your lack of care, your mistake that had made this happen. And then he told me to imagine that I was just a passenger. It wasn't my mistake at all and yet I still found myself clinging to a piece of the wreckage bobbing in the water. Knowing that my life could soon be over, and it wasn't my fault. I had done nothing wrong or nothing to deserve it. What would you think of in those final moments, my grandfather asked me. I told him I didn't know. He told me that a calm would descend and that I would remember all the people I loved and that I wouldn't waste my final precious moments with regrets.'

Anthony's mum burst into tears. Anthony shot up, went straight to her and gave her a hug.

Luke turned to me and said, 'How about we go and take a closer look at the shipwreck?'

'Sure,' I said.

When we had put a little distance between Anthony and Mandy, Luke said, 'I'm sorry about that, mate. Anthony's mum isn't very well.'

'I like Han Solo best,' I said as we were driving back.

'Yes, he is a wonderful character. Have you seen *Raiders of the lost Ark*?' Anthony asked.

'Sure have! I love the Indiana Jones films.'

'Me too!' Anthony said, smiling.

His mum and Luke were chatting quietly in the front. I turned and looked out the window. The sun was shining, I was smiling, the Alfa turned a corner, and the engine began to rev hard. I was having the best time. I looked back and Anthony was looking out his window.

I said, 'It's been a great day, Anthony. Thank you for inviting me.'

'I'm so very pleased to hear that you've enjoyed yourself.'

A car horn started blasting from behind us. I turned and looked out the rear window and saw a big four-wheel drive flashing its high beam headlights on and off at us. Next, it charged passed, swerved in front of us, and then braked suddenly and came quickly to a stop. Luke jammed on the brakes and only just pulled up in time. The driver's door of the four-wheel drive flew open, and a big man dressed in boots, shorts and a blue singlet got out and started charging towards us.

Luke started winding down his window.

Mandy said, 'Be careful, Luke.'

The man slammed his fist down on the bonnet of Luke's car and kept coming, got to Luke's window and shouted. 'Don't you bloody look before pulling out into traffic?'

Luke said, 'I'm sorry.'

'I could have killed you!'

'OK, mate,' Luke said. 'I'm sorry.'

'This piece of junk shouldn't be allowed on the road!'

Luke said, 'I'm sorry, I didn't mean any disrespect.'

The man grabbed Luke's arm through the window. 'Look at yourself in the mirror. You're an idiot!'

Luke didn't look at himself in the mirror. He kept facing the man. He said, 'I'm sorry, I didn't mean any disrespect.'

'You're lucky I'm flying outta the country this week, so I can't get into any trouble. It's the only reason you ain't gettin' hurt.' Then he stormed off, stopping once, pointing at Luke and saying something that I couldn't hear. Then he kicked the front of Luke's car, charged back to his four-wheel drive, climbed in and drove off.

We all sat silent.

Anthony's mum asked, 'Are you OK?'

'Yeah, of course,' Luke said and ran his hand through his hair. 'I'm so sorry about that. I didn't see him.' Then he looked at Anthony and me in the rear-view mirror and said, 'Sorry about that, guys. Some people are idiots. What can you do?' and he smiled at us.

I smiled back at him. I decided right there and then that I wasn't going to hang out with Ryan any more.

I got to school late on Monday. When the bell went for recess, I stayed in the classroom. At lunch, I hung back too. When I was sure everyone would have finished their lunch and would be off on the oval kicking the footy, I went out. But they were all still in the quadrangle. I could see Ryan and his gang crowding around Anthony. I started walking faster towards them. I was almost there when I saw Ryan punch Anthony in the face. Anthony stayed on his feet, but he dropped his lunch box and burst into tears.

I kept approaching. 'Why don't you leave him alone?' I wanted to shout. And I did say it, but it barely came out as a whisper.

'What was that?' Ryan said, turning to face me. 'Ah, where have you been, Stevie?'

'Leave him alone, Ryan,' I said again, my knees trembling, my stomach tight.

And then Ryan was upon me, shoving me in the chest. 'Why? Do you love the fat pig?'

'No!' I said.

He pushed me again, harder, and I lost my footing, I toppled over and fell. I hit the ground, the back of my head first. I felt tears welling in my eyes.

'You gonna cry like your boyfriend?' Ryan sneered. Suddenly, he lurched forward off balance.

'You leave him alone!' I heard Anthony shout.

Ryan shuffled forward until he regained his balance. He steadied himself and turned to face Anthony. I lay there and did nothing but watch. Anthony may have sounded angry and fed up, but he looked terrified. Ryan bared his teeth in a snarl and began charging towards him like a bull. And just like he had done when he had been playing his viola, I saw Anthony close his eyes. But he also clenched his fist and just as Ryan was upon him, he swung it and somehow it connected with the charging Ryan's chin.

Ryan crumbled to the ground. I got to my feet. Ryan's gang fled, leaving only Anthony and me standing above him. My first instinct was to run too. My second was to kick Ryan, hard, and then to keep on kicking him. Anthony had put him down and I didn't want him getting up.

But Anthony had other ideas. I could see his hand was shaking as he bent down and asked him, 'Are you OK?'

Worlds apart

One false step, an unforeseen gust of wind and David could plummet to his death. It is dangerous, retreating to safer ground surely the sanest option. He keeps going, striding along the ridge towards the peak of the snow-capped alp, tightroping the precipice. He feels alive.

All the while, Clare is falling further and further behind, losing sight of him. The sun bakes down on her. She rolls her ankle for the umpteenth time as she staggers on through the flat, dead red earth. There is not a tree in sight, not even on the horizon. They are worlds apart.

Her earth turns to gravel, the gravel turns to stone. In time, she finds herself standing above a craggy rocky gorge. A drought-ravaged river runs within it. She starts down the decline, so steep at points she has to go down on inverted all fours, her hands stretching back behind. The rocks are frying-pan hot, searing her palms. Drenched in sweat, she arrives at the river bed within the gorge. It is parched to the point that it barely flows. She collapses into what is little more than a puddle. She feels as if she is simmering, yet the moisture nourishes, replenishes her, and she drinks. She fills her canteen and drinks again, empties it, fills it, drinks and refills. The relentless sun blazes down, she looks around; there are a few shrubs, several big rocks. She takes shelter beneath the shade of a shrub to rest.

She wakes in the black of night; it is still, she is still, blank, void of emotion. She truly knows that she is finite, yet neither anxiety, nor feelings of futility intrude. There has been, there is and will be; good and bad, restraint and freedom, health and decline. She is far from the start and not at the end. She has an inkling about what she desires for her future, the life she wants. She is beginning to understand herself better.

The onslaught of the sun has returned when next she wakes. She considers waiting for nightfall, but knows she needs to move. She needs to find them. Above all else, she needs momentum. Her renewed strength is quickly sapped as she rescales the cliff face. She stops. Her heart is pounding against her ribs. She drinks from the canteen. 'Slow your breathing,' she tells herself, 'gather yourself, compose yourself and then move on. One step at a time.'

'I cannot find the "Us" that I love,' she thinks. 'Is it gone forever? It's not here, not right now, and I need it. "We" are my plan, my foundation. I want a win-win life for us. Now if they're lost to me, I'm going to have to settle for whatever I'm prepared to take. I'd give anything to possess the ability to change my outlook, my mood, to not stall. I must summon all of my remaining strength. I will spend it on momentum. I have to keep searching.'

Her canteen is empty… She grinds on…this relentless duty to exist… She feels light-headed. 'I will need rest again soon,' she tells herself. 'Breathe and remember, I have only fallen momentarily from grace. We are out of alignment – that is all. A moment, an hour, a day, a year ago, we were true. In those moments, I wanted to live forever.'

But still she can't find them. They are not here. She is out of favour. Her world is black and everything is wrong. And even though they've been here a trillion times before together, she does not trust they will ever find their way back. She never does, she never has. She knows moments can be permanent. 'I cannot endure another moment of this. I want it to be done. Finished. Over. I will stop. Why shouldn't I?'

And then, on the city street ahead of her, David pushing the stroller, slows, comes to a stop and she gains ground. He turns, smiles, and says, 'C'mon.'

And she lets go of the anger, the resentment, her pride, and moves as quickly as fashion allows to their side. She peers into the stroller.

Their son sleeps on. She places her hand upon David's and squeezes it. And like the trillion times before – just like that – they are restored. 'Why do I forget this is all that matters?' she asks herself. 'This is all I've ever truly wanted.'

They walk together, pushing the stroller along the path that turns into their street.

'Why does he get to have it all?' she thinks. 'It's so unfair. I don't care that he makes more. That says more about society than me…'

'Perhaps, if I just went back part-time?' she hears herself say.

David keeps moving forward, pushing the stroller.

'You're not even going to answer me?'

He turns. 'Sorry, haven't I a million times already,' he says and then smiles. 'I just want you to be happy. Whatever you want, Clare.'

'OK, good,' she says, but she can tell. He's getting tired of it.

A cute distraction

The deck dips below then swells above the height of the dock.

Martin leaps aboard, turns, smiles and reaches out his hand to her. 'C'mon,' he says.

She steps out, the deck plunges, she lurches forward, her ankle buckles and she falls into his arms.

'I got you,' he says.

Her head rests against his chest and her eyes settle on the tanned, pinched, wrinkled skin at the intersection of where his bicep meets his forearm.

'She's keen,' calls out a plump, balding man who is one of a group of six grey-haired people already aboard.

The rest erupt into laughter.

'Are you OK?' he asks just loud enough for her to hear.

'Yes,' she says and smiles, freeing herself from his arms and stepping back. 'This boat belongs to you?'

'It's a yacht and yes. I had a crew sail it here.' He escorts her to a seat carved into the fibreglass at the stern. 'I'll be right back.'

She leans back and turns to look out over the vast blue water. Seeing him for the first time in daylight and with his friends has added ten years, maybe double that, to his age.

'For you,' he says on his return, passing her a glass of champagne. He's drinking a beer from the bottle. 'Cheers,' he says as they clink glasses. 'We're going to make for that.'

She looks in the direction of where he's pointing and sees a huge rusting ship on the far side of the bay.

'She ran aground about twenty years ago, lies in shallow water, so we're not sure how close we'll get.'

'Sounds great,' she says. 'I may have slightly sprained my ankle, I'm going to take my shoes off.'

'No, leave them on, I like you in them. I'll be back soon.' He turns and calls to the others, 'Let's do it!'

*

She feels ill in her stomach. The rusting hulk is drawing nearer. It looks both out of place and like it has always been there.

The only other woman aboard, a stylish lady, late forties, perhaps early fifties, is approaching. She smiles and shuffles along to make room for her.

'Hi, I'm Fiona,' she says.

'Cathy,' the older lady says. 'I brought you a refill,' and presents the bottle by lightly waving it in her hand.

'That was kind. Please take a seat,' Fiona says as Cathy fills her glass.

'I won't if it's all the same. I just wanted to have a look at you up close. He's married, you know, and he has a daughter older than you,' she says and then turns and walks back to the others.

*

Fiona puts her hands on the ladder in the cabin to climb back onto the deck. She is out of sight of everyone else above.

'Why's she wearing high heels?' she hears a man say.

She pauses at the bottom of the ladder and thinks it sounds like the fat, balding one.

'Search me,' Martin says.

'She ever been sailing before? Bit overdressed, isn't she?' another man says.

'Did you tell her what we were doing today?' Cathy asks.

'It may have slipped my mind,' Martin says.

The rest laugh.

'Where did you find this one?' It sounds like the fat, balding one again.

33

'Met her last night at the resort bar.'

'She's different,' followed by more laughter.

'Perhaps not up to my usual standards – a cute distraction.'

They all laugh again.

'Oh, Martin, you're terrible,' Cathy says.

She starts climbing the ladder, hoping her ankle won't give.

The colossal, man-made carcass looms above them. They sail from the bright light into its shadow. Nestled in the sand near the bow is an abandoned, derelict, little rowboat.

She sits alone and wonders if it will float. She pictures herself diving from the yacht undetected, swimming to it, heaving it into the water, scrambling over the side and then the gliding of the oars through the water as she silently slips away.

*

He pours her another Scotch and takes a seat beside her on the swing chair on the patio of his resort suite. They are looking out at the bay and beyond that, the ocean. It's dusk, dull and grey. She tries to picture a less cloudy evening, with the setting sun blazing in the sky and it bleeding into the water.

'When I was young, about your age,' he smiles, 'I wasted too many perfect times like this, stressing about what I should or could be doing. Learn from my mistake. The secret is, be in the now. Trust me on that one.'

'What about your wife?' she asks.

'We only have one rule, you and I.' He turns to her. 'You don't ever get to ask about that.'

She says nothing.

They fall silent and continue to stare out at the water.

In time, he places his hand on her knee and says, 'I haven't been very kind to you today, have I? Can you forgive me?'

Later, she closes her eyes. He stinks of drink, sweat and the sea.

Whimpers and roars

'You are being let go,' she says. She has a hard gaunt face, a hawk nose and cruel little eyes. She's late forties, perhaps fifty and obviously keeps herself in shape.

He thinks, there's an air of bitterness about her that doesn't happen overnight; it's unhappiness forged with time. An orphan? Put up for adoption? Certainly overlooked, discarded. Perhaps it came later? A lover dumped her? Something certainly knocked her over and now this is her job, a 'Corporate Downsizing Consultant'. No quips, no small talk, cold, ruthless, straight to it.

'Can I ask why?'

She sighs as if already bored. 'Well, as you know, the business is going through a period of transition, the marketplace is evolving, this industry is moving through an incredible time of innovation.'

'That doesn't really answer my question.'

She smiles. 'I think it does.'

You bitch, you're enjoying this. He sits back, takes a breath.

'So,' she says, 'this is only a courtesy meeting to inform you of how we're intending to move forward. Of course, there will be further opportunities for you to air any grievances you may have.'

He stares at her.

She stares back. 'I have other appointments.'

He looks down at the floor. He's seen other men lose their jobs over the past decade; they were soon forgotten. He's been with this company for nineteen years and he understands that his particular skill is a stale one in the modern corporate landscape. He's forty-four years old and suspects it could all unravel very quickly for him from here.

'Excuse me,' she says, 'I need you to leave.'

I've always been a competitor; do something. He looks back up and locks eyes with her. He slowly stands holding her gaze. He breaks off, turns and walks out of the office.

From over his shoulder, he hears her say, 'You can leave the door.'

He heads straight to his desk and gathers a few things, mainly his personal items, puts them into his briefcase and leaves the building.

He arrives home, drops his briefcase onto the floor by the sofa and a takeaway pizza onto the coffee table, picks up both remote controls and turns on the TV. He removes his already loosened tie and drapes it over an armchair.

He walks into the kitchen, washes and dries his hands, opens the cabinet and removes a glass. From the freezer he lifts out the ice tray, twists it, and several ice blocks pop free. He places them in the glass. He opens and reaches to the rear of another cabinet and removes a dusty unopened bottle of Scotch. It was presented to him after ten years with the company. He opens it, pours a generous measure, takes a sip, shrugs and carries the glass and the bottle back into the living room and places them on the coffee table.

He sits, chewing on a piece of pizza, watching the news. The reporter is speaking about a zoo in some Asian city that is in financial trouble, over a montage of emaciated monkeys, bears and tigers. As the reporter signs off, the footage is of a lion in a cage, his mane limp, ribs showing through his sides as he slowly prowls around. The lion turns and faces the camera as the story ends.

He picks up the remote control and changes the channel.

His phone buzzes on the table. He picks it up and looks at the screen.

It's a text from Charlotte. 'Don't forget to pick up some dinner. I'm out with the boys for a girls' night. Love you, C xxx.'

He smiles. 'The boys' are Joel and Eric – he doesn't get invited on these nights out any more. It doesn't bother him. He texts back, 'Hadn't forgotten, have a great night. Say hi to Joel and Eric for me. Love you.' He presses send and goes and gets some more ice from the kitchen.

He's eaten three slices of pizza and is onto his fourth Scotch when the phone buzzes.

It's Charlotte again. 'I have the best news! Eric and Joel are adopting a baby! We're going to head out to celebrate! Don't wait up, I'll crash here tonight, the boys send you big hugs and kisses! Love you, C xxx.'

A football panel show he enjoys watching comes on. It's hosted by ex-players who he grew up watching play. They get down to business pretty quickly tonight. They are having a rather heated discussion about the state of a new recruit's mental health. The camera zooms in on one of the panellists; he looks really old.

He pours another drink; he doesn't get ice.

It occurs to him that he hasn't replied to Charlotte's message, so he rereads her last text. For a reason he can't quite put his finger on, he doesn't know what to say.

Is it because Eric and Joel are adopting a baby? No, I don't care what they do.

Is it that Charlotte won't be coming home? Yeah maybe, I want to see her.

But there is something more.

He puts the phone down on the couch, picks up the remote and starts flicking through the channels.

…a roar…fangs exposed…claws slashing the air and furred skin… blood…two male lions in the wild are tearing each other to pieces. It goes on and on, it is brutal. The narrator finally speaks. 'The young challenger defeats the old lion. The old lion will be banished from the pride. If he survives his wounds, he will live out his days in exile.'

He turns off the TV and the room is suddenly dim, still and quiet. He pictures the hard, cruel features of the woman who sacked him. He remembers she smiled.

She has jeopardised my security, my happiness, my future and I said nothing.

I wish she had been a man.

He is not now, nor has he ever been a violent person, but if she were a man, right now, he would hunt him down and beat him to death with his bare hands. He understands now too why he felt uneasy about Charlotte's last text. He is losing his grip and is getting shut out, excluded from his world. That banished old lion fought to the end, went down roaring.

I said nothing today.

He leans forward and puts his face in his hands, then runs his fingers through his receding, thinning hair. He starts fantasising about what he could have said in that office…

Beyond what we'd like to be true, there is a law of nature… We are animals…a kingdom of man. So go against nature all you like… Build your ivory towers on a foundation of dreams of equality…lobby the stakeholders in your parliaments, delude yourself things can be different in your utopian cities… When you finally place your feet back on terra firma, before you start tearing my life down, remember where you have come from – for you too were powerless once. Remember how that felt and how angry it made you. Before you get too comfortable in your dream city, be sure to take a step back into the jungle. There you'll find nothing has changed… There is law – like gravity…and all your delusions of how things should be, dreams and protests, fall away…for you do not stand a chance against the lion…the king of the jungle… He is bigger and stronger. And when toe to toe, all you will do, is what you have always done – run. Just like you did when you were the scared child, caught in a lie. And like then, when you wished things could be different, your warping and manipulating of the fact, doesn't change truth… All the time you have been building your city, the lion has slept…if he's hungry when he wakes, he will kill and eat.

His phone buzzes again, he picks it up.

Charlotte, 'Where are you?'

He types, 'I wish I were a lion,' and stops…

Do I? This isn't a jungle, and they cage lions in cities.

His anger dissolves. It never lasts long these days, even if he wants it to, he cannot sustain it. He just wants sleep now, for this day to be done. He deletes what he has written and types, 'Sorry, I mustn't have pressed send before. Congrats to the boys, have a great night and stay safe. Love you.' He presses send, turns the phone off and tosses it onto the coffee table.

He looks at the pizza box and the two-thirds-empty bottle of Scotch in the dim light.

I'll clean all of this up tomorrow.

The pit bull

The old lady is thinking of the last time she came walking through the outskirts of the town en route to the river. She was lost in her thoughts, taking a shortcut down a laneway lined with tall metal sheds. One had a tractor and other farm machinery secured in the yard behind a padlocked wire gate and fence.

She had heard the guttural growl before she saw the muscular shoulders and the pink watery eyes of the albino pit bull behind the wire… hunched, priming to pounce, it charged all the while shooting its machine gun bark closer and closer to within a few metres of her.

Like her mother, she had always believed in God and she prayed.

Suddenly, the beast had reared up onto its hind legs. Its rampage had been abruptly halted when the thick metal chain attached to the collar around its neck pulled taut. It continued its blitzkrieg of hatred at her as she hastened her step and thanked God.

The summer came and, with it, the irritation and anxiety of the 'high fire danger' false alarms had resumed for another season. Each day on the way out the front door, on the way to the relative safety of the nearby city, she would take a small suitcase full of the bare essentials: her best outfit, a photo album, favourite books, personal papers, her sponge bag, et cetera, et cetera, and put it in the boot of her car.

The black skies are six months past now, the threat is gone. Only the devastation remains, and a new knowing that she is out the other side of a time that would never be forgotten and will go on requiring to be endured.

The fires had reached, yet had not completely destroyed, the town. She is one of the lucky ones; her house still stands.

This day, for the first time, she finds herself walking down that same laneway on the way to the river. She looks around at the charcoal remains, reminiscent in a way, of grainy footage of 1945 Berlin from a World War II documentary she once saw.

Rain has come and gone since, green shoots sprout in the black earth, time passes, scars heal. She almost doesn't recognise the melted and blackened ruins of the tractor and the other machinery. Only the tall metal posts remain of the fence; the sheds have drunkenly collapsed in on themselves. They will be bulldozed soon too, she thinks, not a high priority. And then she sees it, brown and coiling on the ground against the charred, black earth. The thick chain.

And she remembers that tethered beast, all its grunt and spite and vile…

Was it saved? Or couldn't its people get back? And if they couldn't, or didn't, did that most-feared creature, that chained caged monster, sense the danger coming?

In those final moments, was it frantically trying to free itself? Or did it whimper for its mother? Or did it at last understand its fate? That all the anger and fury and savagery it could muster wasn't going to save it. And that all of that anger and fury and vitriol had been a complete waste of time and energy and effort, all along.

Battery life

He is floating on his back in the lagoon that flows into the tropical sea, looking up at a cloudless blue sky. I'm not expected anywhere for the next three days, he thinks. I deserve this. A towering coconut palm arrives in his field of vision. I must be drifting closer to the shore. He smiles to himself and drifts on.

He sees the old man early the next morning. He is looking through binoculars, in the shade of a tree, panning left to right, focused. Brad had been following the old track that ran along the cliff, dressed in shorts, a well-worn and long since retired business shirt, his old rust-coloured terry towelling hat and a pair of canvas shoes. He wonders what the other man is searching for, when the binoculars stop panning. The old man appears to have found whatever it is. Brad looks down into a sunlit bay too, but nothing stands out.

The old man sets off along the track in the direction that Brad had been heading. So Brad follows, staying a respectful distance behind. Further along the cliff face, the old man turns onto a path that heads inland. The path soon begins to gradually descend. Palm trees stretch all around to the sky.

In time, the track becomes less discernible, debris of leaves, twigs and small branches make it harder to distinguish from its surroundings. The sun breaks through the canopy adding a mottled, speckled, sepia light effect. The day is warm, and Brad is sweating, yet the deeper he descends, the cooler it gets. Birds constantly chatter. He can hear his own laboured breath and the constant roar of the surf.

The descent grows far steeper and a little soggy underfoot as the terrain changes. Now he is walking through waist-high ferns. He has become aware of the sound of flowing water close by; he sees the creek.

Up ahead, the old man has set a course parallel with it and continues his march. Brad watches the water trickle over the moss-covered rocks. He breathes in and out deeply and closes his eyes and opens them again, so he doesn't lose his footing.

He turns a corner and is hit by the breeze. He strides on and soon arrives on the sand of a beach within a bay, that he is sure is the same one he viewed from the clifftop. Waves roar through the heads and crash on the beach.

The old man, far ahead, is struggling out, gingerly stepping over the rocks that are at the base of the head on the left-hand side and that stretch out beyond it. He is being buffeted by the wind and the sea, but he keeps going. He stops from time to time and appears to study the rocks on which he treads. The old man keeps moving further out and is soon no longer in sight, obscured by the cliff face of the headland.

Brad takes a seat on the sand and waits.

In time, the old man reappears, cautiously navigating his way back along the rocks. 'Ahoy there,' he calls out when he reaches the sand.

'Hello,' Brad replies, stands and begins walking towards him. 'Did you find what you were looking for?'

'No, afraid not. If there's a shipwreck out there, I can't see it,' the old man says.

'A shipwreck?'

'Yes, legend has it. The remains of a shipwreck lie in a pool amongst the rocks. It's only accessible at low tide.' Up close, his face is old, under a beaten hat, with white whiskers sprouting from cheek to chest, with purple nose and yellow teeth. 'I thought that I'd spied her from above just before. It was just a mirage, I'm afraid.'

'Still, sounds exciting.'

'Just an old man and his folly,' he says, removing a hip flask from a buttoned pocket on his shorts. 'She carried a treasure apparently.'

'I can think of worse dreams to chase than treasure.'

'I'm not going to argue there,' the man says, then, takes a swig from his flask. 'But enough of me. What brings you out here?'

'Holiday, I needed to get away. Escape my life on the mainland for a while.'

'I get that. Work or a woman?'

'Both, I think.'

'Well, I'm sorry to hear that.'

'A bit of time and all will be well, I'm sure.'

'Don't take too long. Work doesn't matter, but she does. Then again, it takes two. Did she consider coming with you?'

'Sorry, I think you misunderstood. She's back at the cabin. It was her idea for us to come here.'

'So you're in paradise and you're standing around talking to me?'

'Yeah, I should be getting back.'

'Good luck.'

But Brad doesn't go. He just stands there.

'Are you all right, son?' the old man asks.

'No, no, I don't think I am.'

'What is it?'

'That's what I'm trying to figure out. I don't know. I think, I just want more.'

'More?' The old man says shaking his head. 'You've got a job, obviously enough money to get away and she came with you.'

'Is that enough?'

'Learn from my mistake. I'm an old man searching for treasure. Not because I never had any, but because I lost it. Most people end up misplacing what they truly value somewhere along the way. So I'm out here trying to salvage something. If you ask me, your treasure is waiting for you back at the cabin and you're out here searching for more? Careful, you very well could be in the process of losing it – not finding it.'

Brad smiles. 'Thanks for the advice,' he says. 'You might even be right.'

'Of course I am. On your way.'

'Well, I hope you find some treasure.'

The old man smiles. 'Well, it's too late for that. But perhaps I'll get lucky.'

'We're returning home too soon,' Brad says, walking with Emma close to the waterline where it's easier to tread; you don't sink into the sand. 'I'm not ready.'

'Look,' Emma says, and he turns to where she's pointing.

Not five metres from the shore and seemingly out of nowhere, two fins have appeared and are swimming towards the shore. They get closer and then turn and start heading in the same direction. Brad originally had thought they were sharks but can now clearly see they are in fact dolphins. He reaches out, takes Emma's hand and the four of them carry on in convoy.

Then it hits him. This is what he needed this trip. Some sign, a knowing, a restoration, a reminder of the knowing that you only have one life, you only have one real choice – you must go on. He's been focusing on the wrong things. The old man was right. Life, good and bad, is unforeseen. Some bad things are coming, and some things are coming that just make it totally worth it. He doesn't want to miss them…and more than that, he wants to share them.

'This is where I belong,' he says, 'with you.'

Emma moves closer and rests her head on his shoulder. They stop walking, the dolphins swim on.

He turns to look at her. 'How are you feeling, Em?' he asks.

'Recharged,' she says and gives his hand a squeeze, and then they too continue on their way.

Fever

'Sir, I'm afraid you will still need to be picked up,' the pretty, young lady doctor says.

'Well, we've got a problem then,' he replies, lying on a hospital trolley, a drip already in his arm, wearing nothing but the backless gown with which they had supplied him. 'There is no one.'

The doctor smiles a tired smile and nods, turns, tugs open the curtain and leaves.

He wakes to the sound of rushing water. Something is missing, a sensation, the constant dull throb of the engines is gone. We're sinking, he knows. He is below deck; he has to move. He leaps from his bunk and splashes into water that has already risen above his ankles. He steps out into the passageway and wades through the rising water, climbs the stairs, and soon arrives out on the deck. It is deserted. He heads straight to the side rail, steps over it and dives head first into the sea. His body plunges deeper and deeper. Eventually, he stops descending, pauses, then slowly begins kicking back towards the surface. He breaks through and gasps in the brisk night air. He treads water, composes himself and looks around. A lone palm tree casts a silhouette against the star-filled night sky. He swims towards it and doesn't stop until his hands strike sand. He stands and staggers through the water; he arrives on a tiny island that has barely enough landmass to support the palm tree. Safe for now, settled with his back against the tree, he looks to the ship. It appears to be fully intact before him. And then, seemingly without warning, it rapidly begins to break up and slide beneath the surface. Soon, it is completely gone from view.

An alarm is going off, close, in his ear, slightly above him, to his right. His eyes snap open, his heart is belting, he feels fire beneath his flesh, he's struggling to catch his breath. Hurried footsteps…hushed, urgent voices approach…orbit…the alarm stops…someone is speaking at him, '…emergency surgery…complications…fever…'

The voices grow calmer…the footsteps are now retreating. He is lying on his back, head turned facing a machine which has red and green lights that silently blink. In the dim light, he can see its tentacles reaching out to him, piercing his skin, invading his blood. He senses he shouldn't move. He understands that he is in a hospital bed. A blackness circles, creeps closer, overtakes him…

The sun rises, the sun sets. He is still there, with his back against the palm tree on the tiny island, the vast cloudless sky and ocean are all that is to be seen in any direction. He is unnoticed, forgotten, exhausted, sunburnt, thirsty, powerless. 'I have done nothing to deserve this,' he rasps. 'This isn't my fault.'

Life is beginnings, middles and endings, he is thinking as he lies in the darkness still tethered to the machine the following night. He has long known that if you live long enough, they start overlapping. Until now, his thinking has always involved an element of projecting onto a distant future. But if he dies, if he ends here, that changes. The unresolved issues of his life will stay unresolved. Unchased dreams will be left unchased. He had some good times, some bad – game over.

He pictures himself marooned on that island, on that vast sea, and it makes him angry. A new perspective is dawning. Until now, he's been a passenger, going with the flow, trying to play nice, to be good, to contribute. He's been willing to compromise, and he thought it a reasonable price to pay to belong. In this spirit, he has sacrificed, gone without, been there for others. He thought that was the deal. But when the time arrived when he needed support, he found himself alone. In hindsight, he can see that he had forged contracts with souls who never intended living up to their responsibilities to him. He can see too that it was folly of him to think that life worked that way. 'A river only flows in one direction,' he whispers. 'If I get out of this, changes will be made.'

The morning linen change is complete, he has showered and is sitting up in bed. The doctor will be here soon, and he wants to be awake. He knows he is getting stronger, and he wants to tell her, 'Let me out of here, out of this bed. I want to feel the sun, rain, nature on my skin. I'm ready to begin.'

He steps out onto the street and a warm breeze strikes his cheek. From this day forth, I will be the captain of my own ship, he thinks. This way, I and I alone will set the course. I will decide who and what belongs in my life. What works and what gets thrown overboard. The time has come for new horizons, to take control – to put my happiness first. But where to begin?

He had agreed to get a taxi straight home, but he's not ready to go home just yet. He has spent a lifetime doing what he's told, what's expected of him. It's a beautiful, sunny day and he wants to be out in it for a time. He pictures himself as the captain behind his ship's wheel, sailing the ocean.

These tumultuous waters have been navigated… I know the seas can be cruel… I will need to batten down the hatches in stormy times… find safe harbour…there is no such thing as clear sailing. Right now, I will enjoy these calm waters, the wind and sun at my back. This is my second chance, a new beginning; I want to get it right. In its simplest form, life is just a series of moments. I intend to fill mine with as many good ones as I can. I will live a good life, my life, I will enjoy it.

There's a café he knows not far from here, down a cobbled stone laneway, where the staff are friendly. The lady customers will be wearing summer dresses and the men business suits and ties without jackets. The thought of sitting with a coffee, in those surrounds, being part of that, creates a pleasing picture in his mind. Finally, an island of my choosing, he thinks, as he sets sail.

Exits

My mother and I had moved back in with my grandparents by then. My grandmother was a beautifully dressed lady and she loved her garden. She never talked about my mother's illness. I watched her once, on her knees quietly attending to a garden bed. She must have felt safe, alone, unobserved, because without warning, she slumped forward and her body began heaving. I was about to run to her aid, when she began pounding the earth with clenched fists. I stayed where I was. Eventually, she stopped sobbing, removed a tissue from the sleeve of her shirt and dabbed at her eyes and cheeks. She then resumed her work.

I never knew my father. I was eleven years old when I met Luke. He was twenty-six. My mother was thirty and her skin had a greenish tinge that had nothing to do with what was killing her. But it was the reason the other kids at school called her 'The Hulk'. She was slight of build. Luke thought she was beautiful and he told her often, which made her smile. I liked him for that. On the weekends, we'd go and stay at his place. He had a small flat above a strip of shops. There was an Indian restaurant a few doors down and we would eat there most Saturday nights or get takeaways and take them back to his flat and watch TV. One night through the week, my mother would go and stay with Luke without me.

He wore a black leather Jacket. I thought it was cool and he drove an old dark blue Alfa Romeo. He was very proud of that car. He would boast of 'the note of the engine – they call it European exhaust'. When a traffic light would turn green, he would always charge off the line first. The engine was loud and it sounded like a racing car revving high through the gears. It felt like we were going very fast, but the other cars would always quickly catch us and overtake.

The three of us and my best friend from primary school had a picnic for my twelfth birthday down by the bay. It had been a long but happy drive in the Alfa Romeo. It was a sunny day and there was a rusted brown shipwreck poking out of the water, not far out to sea. Luke and I were fascinated by it. Luke used up a whole roll of film on his camera that afternoon. Every shot had my mother in it. The rest were a combination of my mother and me, or my mother, my friend and me. Most of them had the rusty old shipwreck in the background.

After my mother was gone, he would still come and visit us from time to time and take me out for the day. We would go for lunch at the pub, he would drink a couple of beers and I would drink lemon squash. We played pool once. I was terrible at it; he wasn't much better. The game took forever. We never played again. We went and saw a movie a few times. I don't really remember what we talked about. He would crack jokes. He probably asked how school was going. I remember thinking he was trying too hard.

One Saturday, he arrived to pick me up with a black eye. My grandparents, Luke and I sat out in the summer house drinking coffee in fine china cups. My grandmother said nothing about his eye and still let me go with him.

My mother had been an amateur violinist, a good one. I play the viola. He came and saw a couple of my concerts when I was at school. He sat with my grandmother. I only recall going back into his flat once in that time. For some reason, I ended up in his bedroom. A photo of my mother and me and the shipwreck sat on his bedside table.

I had not long turned eighteen and was out for dinner with a group of friends. There was a very loud table of eight diners in the restaurant. They were rude to the staff, constantly demanding more drinks. Luke was among them. He had his arm around some tarty cheap blonde. She spent a lot of the evening attempting to eat his ear.

When I got into uni, I moved out of my grandparents' house for the final time. I don't know if Luke still dropped around after that. My grandmother never said so if he did.

I had recently landed a job in orchestral management when my grandfather died. Luke was at the wake, head bowed, nodding in conversation with my grandmother. He was wearing his old leather jacket, but it didn't look cool any more – it was an inappropriate thing for him to have worn. He had that look of a man who drank more than he should. My grandmother gave him a hug. He saw me, smiled and began walking towards me. I turned and walked to another group of people and began a conversation.

An email arrived from him out of the blue. 'Travelling around Europe for the first time in years. Saw this and was reminded of happy days. I hope life is treating you well, Luke.'

There was an attachment. I opened it. It was a photo of a shipwreck, sitting in shallow water in some European country. He didn't say which one. That kind of detail didn't occur to him. I didn't reply.

When I turned thirty-three, the same age my mother was when she died, I went to his old flat. No sign of the Alfa Romeo. I knocked on the door. The man who answered knew nothing of him.

I took a job with another orchestra in another city. I had printed off the shipwreck email and had kept it amongst my personal papers. I found it, took his email address from it and wrote him a long message. I was feeling homesick. My internet server replied immediately, 'Delivery Status Notification (Failure)'.

More years have passed. My wife and our daughter and I are back in town for a visit. We are out walking around the old suburb on our way to the park, our daughter in her stroller. It's a sunny autumn day, there are joggers passing us in both directions. Arriving at the park, we turn onto the path. We pass by families gathered around the community play equipment, fathers and sons kicking footballs, groups of friends throwing frisbees. Soon the barbecues will be getting fired up.

In the distance, I see Luke with a lady walking briskly towards us. They are not in tracksuits, but the pace they are moving at suggests exercise. She says something and he laughs and his head tilts back like it used to. They pass straight by us, chatting happily to each other. He looks healthy, relaxed.

I say quietly to my wife, 'That was Luke.'

'*The* Luke?' she replies.

'Yes.'

Lying in bed that night in the dark, whispering so we don't wake our daughter in her cot at the end of the bed, my wife asks, 'Are you going to try and track him down again?'

'I don't think so,' I say.

'Why not?'

'Why would I? We're not related, we're not friends. He was good to my mother and to me and to my grandmother a long time ago. I only ever wanted to know that he was happy and doing OK. He looked like he was today.'

We lie silent, but I feel that something has changed between us. That 'sometime void' has begun and I don't want it to now, not on this trip.

'Did I say something wrong?' I ask.

She sighs and whispers, 'Wouldn't it be nice to thank him?'

Worth the wait

Luke takes a sip from his latte and looks around the airport bar. Two large women in their mid-thirties are drinking beer, sitting on barstools at a high table, chatting. The slightly smaller of the two has a nose ring and several ear piercings. She is wearing a tank top and shorts from which spills ample flesh, expansively adorned with a tattooist's ink. The other, who is facing away from him, suddenly erupts into cackles of laughter.

The slightly smaller one catches him looking at them. The warmth reserved for her friend dissolves from her face. She eyeballs him and snarls, 'What are you lookin' at?'

He turns away. She says something else that he doesn't hear.

Another day, another time, he would have engaged her. Back then, he had mythologised life as a war and himself as a fighter. Arguing, standing his ground, energised him, motivated him. Eventually, he grew tired of that world view. Too many hollow victories, too many defeats, too many stalemates. It stopped working. These days, he sees things differently. Perhaps a little pragmatically, he concedes, he's gathered and experienced the things that truly matter to him. He's arrived at a place where he has achieved. He loves his trophies. He's philosophical about valued things lost or misplaced.

He checks the time on his phone. Ginny's flight is due to land in twenty minutes. She has been away for ten days. He had deliberately arrived at the airport early. He didn't want to be late and he was sick of rattling around their apartment alone. It's time to move. He takes a final sip of coffee, stands, pushes the chair back under the table and glances one last time at the two fat women. They've resumed their conversation. He thinks briefly about the one who had snapped at him.

She is just a hurt, damaged, lost, angry person presenting an aggressive face to the world. Lashing out at me isn't going to change a thing.

Strolling past the shops on the way to the gate where Ginny's plane will be arriving, he feels nervous, excited. He has missed her. Before Ginny, his life had come to resemble a puzzle he was incapable of solving. Somewhere along the way, he had begun to compare his existence to that of an empty passenger train. Destined to go around and around on the city loop in his mind forever 'Stopping all stations'.

I only get one life. Am I wasting it? Am I searching for meaning, happiness, in the wrong places? A lot of people end up misplacing what they truly value somewhere along the way. What do I truly value? How did I get it so wrong? What am I missing?

Within months of their relationship beginning, everything had changed. He realises now that he had remained suspicious of his new-found contentment, the absence of restlessness, his joy, for far longer than he needed to have. He believes now, too, that he had not been wrong to perceive his life, at a level, as a puzzle. Ginny, it turns out, had simply been the missing piece.

Arriving at the gate, he glances up at the Arrival and Departures screen to double check that he's come to the right place and notices for the first time that her flight has been delayed by an hour. A vice clamps his heart, his spirit plummets and all the goodwill for this life and for his fellow man that he was feeling, evaporates. He reminds himself that this is beyond his control, but it doesn't help. He feels his blood belting through his veins and the old fighter within him wants blood. He considers charging straight back to the bar and telling that 'large woman' exactly what he is looking at.

His anger never lasts long these days. Even if he wants it to, he cannot sustain it, it exhausts him. Before, when things didn't go his way, when he perceived the universe to be conspiring to disrespect him, he would lash out, strike back, go to war. Demonstrate to the rude, the ignorant, those incapable of empathy, that for every action, there is a reaction. While a part of him still believes this to be true, he understands that the 'large woman' being rude and the plane being delayed are unrelated. Further, lashing out at her, even just in his own head, achieves nothing.

He slumps into a seat at the lounge and exhales. Increasingly, it seems to him that, in moments like this, he is just a soul incapable of viewing the world through any other prism than – this life ends. That is the fate of all things. Now is all he has, all he gets. Hence, he knows that he is not wrong to hate the circumstances which result in his 'now' being wasted. This moment, like all others in his life, is fleeting. Time doesn't speed up, but that doesn't mean it isn't running out.

The starving hunt for food, the thirsty for drink, the lonely search for love, the restless answers. And he has been all of those things and more. He once mythologised himself a fighter and he wasn't wrong to. There were wars, causes worth fighting for then. As the fog of youth cleared, in time he came to realise that all he was really searching for, striving for, was to live a happy life. He understands now that anger and happiness, achievement and loss have two impacts on his psyche; they are both fleeting and accumulative.

He thinks of Ginny and their life together and knows there is no happier life for him. That is all that truly matters. He understands, too, that believing this will not immunise him from life's follies. They remain unavoidable. Further, certain disrespects will have to be endured, but so many can be dismissed. He gets to choose. He doesn't want to be a fighter any more and he doesn't have to be. How can you fight the peace? Why would you want to? He wanted a happy life and he has won. I love our life, he tells himself. This is only a minor delay. She will be here soon.